This Treasury
belongs to

..........Vaila..........

A
Treasury of
Make
Believe

This is a Parragon book
This edition published in 2000

Parragon
Queen Street House
4 Queen Street
Bath BA1 1HE UK

Produced by
The Templar Company plc
Pippbrook Mill
London Road
Dorking, Surrey RH4 1JE UK

Printed and bound in Italy
ISBN 0 75253 472 6

A Treasury of Make Believe

p

Contents

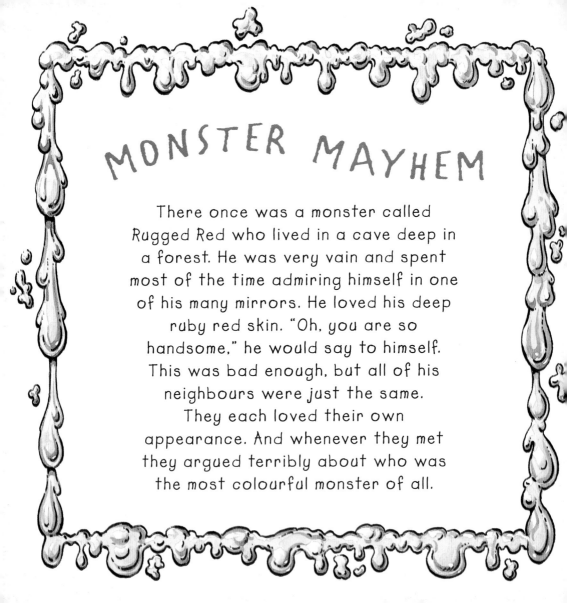

MONSTER MAYHEM

There once was a monster called Rugged Red who lived in a cave deep in a forest. He was very vain and spent most of the time admiring himself in one of his many mirrors. He loved his deep ruby red skin. "Oh, you are so handsome," he would say to himself. This was bad enough, but all of his neighbours were just the same. They each loved their own appearance. And whenever they met they argued terribly about who was the most colourful monster of all.

Paul Gamble.

Now, one day, Gorgeous Green, who was the Great Governor of the monsters, got fed up with listening to all the arguing and fighting. So she thought of a plan to put a stop to it, once and for all. She decided to have a party and invited all the monsters. Everyone was very excited. They were soon busy getting ready — washing and brushing, polishing and shining — and arguing more loudly than ever about who would look the best at the party!

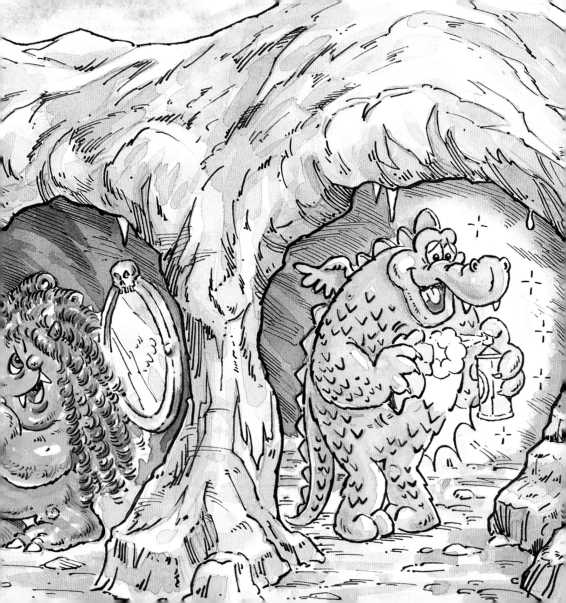

Gorgeous Green had been busy too. She had put up balloons, streamers, and lots of mirrors. There were lovely things to eat, party games and a monster band. And as each monster arrived they were given a strange sparkling drink.

But the monsters were not interested in the food, the party games or the music. They were too busy looking at their own reflections and arguing about who was the nicest colour! The monsters were so interested in themselves that they had forgotten how to have fun with each other.

Which is why Gorgeous Green had given them a magic potion. The strange sparkling drink soon turned every single monster grey - even Gorgeous Green herself! When they saw what had happened they were angry and upset - whatever was going on?

The band stopped playing as Gorgeous Green stood to speak. "I invited you here to have fun, but you are all too busy arguing. I thought that if everyone looked the same, there would be nothing more to argue about. Now you can enjoy the party, have fun and make friends!"

One by one the monsters realised how silly they had been. After that they had a wonderful afternoon. They played, and danced and ate and laughed and sang. Gorgeous Green was very happy. Her plan had worked.

"Now you can see that being different colours doesn't matter, and nobody is better than anyone else," she said. "Since you have learnt this important lesson, I think it's time to change back to our original colours." She gave them each another drink, and their colours returned. But this time they did not argue. They carried on with the party late into the night. Nobody wanted to go home. They all stayed and had fun instead!

Ned the Gnome

Ned the Gnome spent the morning jumping
into sticky mud puddles. He tried to tell
himself he loved mud, but he didn't really
... not even a little bit. Feeling fed up, Ned
sat wondering what he was going to do.
"Excuse me," said a voice behind him,
"but why don't you smell?"
Ned turned to see a little brown rabbit.
"Why should I smell?" asked Ned.
"You're a gnome, aren't you?" said the
rabbit. "All gnomes are rude, dirty and
smell horrible."

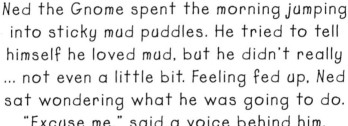

"That's the problem," said Ned. "I don't like
dirt and mud and I hate being rude to people."
"I see," said the rabbit –
"A clean, polite gnome.
Doesn't that make life a bit
difficult with the other gnomes?"
"Of course," replied Ned.
"The other gnomes laugh at me."
"Follow me then,"
said the rabbit.
"I know where there are
some clean gnomes."
And the rabbit hopped
off with Ned following
closely behind.

Soon they came to a house, the sort that humans live in. Beside a pond in the garden were some very clean gnomes. "Hello, I'm Ned," said Ned to a gnome who was holding a tiny fishing rod.

"Sshh," hissed the gnome. "We only talk at night." And he sat staring ahead, refusing to say another word. Ned looked at the rabbit and shrugged. "Let's come back later," he said.

Later, when the stars were out, Ned tried again. He explained his problem and said that if they were all nice, clean, polite gnomes, then he would like to join them please.

The gnome thought for a while. "O.K.," he said eventually. "Go and sit over there," and he pointed to a space between two other gnomes. Ned did as he was told. "Hello," said Ned. "My name is Ned. What's yours?" "Sshh," said one of the gnomes. "We aren't allowed to talk much in case we disturb the fish." Ned sat quietly for a while, then got up to stretch his legs. "Sit still," hissed the other gnome. "We aren't allowed to move, we might disturb the fish." Later, a gust of wind blew one of the gnomes over, but no one went to help him.

"Why doesn't he get up? Is he hurt?"
Ned asked in surprise. "No," came the reply.
"He's a plastic gnome that belongs to the
humans." Ned looked
round and thought
to himself,
"I can't tell
the difference."

"Don't you get bored?" Ned asked the
gnome to his right.
"Of course not. It is our job to watch
over the fish. We have to protect them."
Ned sat for a while longer. At the far end
of the garden he could see his friend the
rabbit waiting. Quietly he left the pond
and went over to her.
"I have never been so bored in all my life,"
he told the rabbit.
"My friends might be rude and smelly, but
at least they're not boring."
"Time to go home, I think," said the rabbit.

When Ned arrived home, the other gnomes made a big fuss of him. He told them about his adventure and they were very upset that he had nearly left them. So they made a deal. No one would mind if Ned was clean, sweet smelling and polite, as long as Ned did not mind that the others were sometimes rude, and almost always dirty and smelly. After that Ned was never tempted to leave his gnome home again, although he did sometimes go for long walks with his special friend the rabbit.

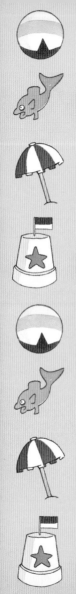

A Perfect Day

Can you think of a better way to spend a hot and sunny summer's day, than having a picnic on the beach? Big Bear and his friends thought it was a great idea, and were very excited when they set off for the seaside in Bill Badger's shiny new car. The sun was beating down, and the sky was clear and blue. But just then there was a loud rumble.

"Oh no," said Percy Pig. "Thunder!"

"No, just my stomach," blushed Big Bear.

"I'm getting hungry. Is it far?"

"Nearly there," said Bill.

By the time they arrived at the beach everyone was feeling hot and sticky. "Thank goodness we brought the umbrella," said Percy. "We're going to need some shade in this heat!"

"Let's go for a swim to cool down!" said Morris Mouse. While the others raced off for a dip in the sea, Big Bear stayed behind to set up the umbrella and unpack the picnic. But the others had such fun playing in the sea, that they were gone for ages. "Perhaps I'll just have a sandwich while I'm waiting," said Big Bear to himself, as his stomach rumbled again...

Much later, Big Bear woke with a start.
Something wet was dripping on his face.
He opened his eyes to see the others back
from their swim, and looking at him sternly.
"Hey, watch out, you're splashing me!" he said.
"It's not us," said Percy, crossly.
"It's raining. What's happened to the
umbrella, and where is our picnic?"
"Oh dear me," said Big Bear.
The others had been gone so
long that Big Bear had eaten all
of the picnic, then fallen
asleep against the umbrella
and broken it. And now it
was raining!
"What a dreadful day this
is turning out to be," said
Olive Owl, with a groan.
"Let's hurry up and go home."

By the time they were ready to leave the sun had started to shine again. "I'm really very sorry about the picnic," said Big Bear," but I'm such a hungry bear! And I think I know just how to cheer you all up!" In no time they were back at Big Bear's house having tea in the shade of the big oak tree in his garden. "At least this is one umbrella that you can't break, Big Bear!" joked his little friend Morris Mouse, and everyone laughed. And as they munched happily they all agreed it had been a great day after all.

GOBLINS IN THE GUTTER

Goblins are small and ugly creatures who never wash and smell terrible. They live in dark, damp places, and only like to come out at night. Worst of all they hate everyone and everything. Goblins can't stand happy people. Which is why they didn't like Poppy...

The goblins lived in a drain in the road outside Poppy's house in Acacia Avenue. They had moved there when their home at Maple Close was dug up. The jolly workmen who sang songs and told jokes were more than they could stand. So they packed up and moved. But they soon realised this was a big mistake.

Poppy was always happy. She had a nice *mum* and dad and a big brother called Fred, who she thought was great. She loved school, and always worked hard for her teacher.

"It makes me feel sick," said Gruel, the oldest, grumpiest goblin, "every time I see Whatshername skipping along to school with a big smile on her face."

"Let's sort her out," said a fat goblin called Squelch. "If we can't stop her smiling, I'm a pixie!"

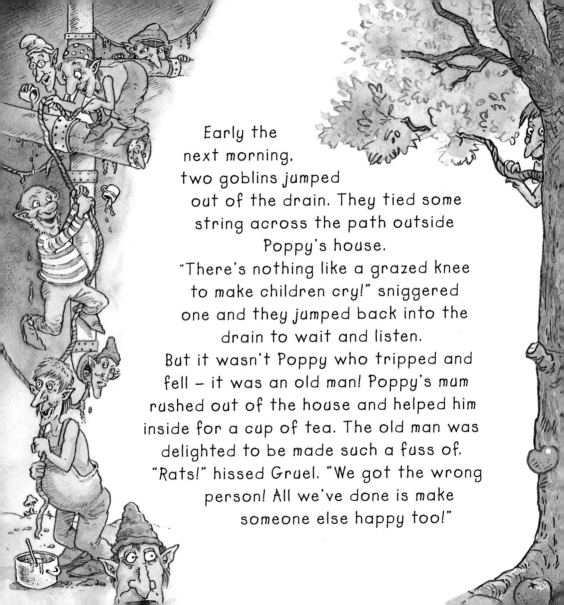

Early the
next morning,
two goblins jumped
out of the drain. They tied some
string across the path outside
Poppy's house.
"There's nothing like a grazed knee
to make children cry!" sniggered
one and they jumped back into the
drain to wait and listen.
But it wasn't Poppy who tripped and
fell – it was an old man! Poppy's mum
rushed out of the house and helped him
inside for a cup of tea. The old man was
delighted to be made such a fuss of.
"Rats!" hissed Gruel. "We got the wrong
person! All we've done is make
someone else happy too!"

That night, Squelch crept along
the drains, up the pipes and
through the plughole into the
kitchen sink in Poppy's house.
There on the table was her
lunchbox, which Poppy's mum
packed the night before.

He took the cheese out
of her sandwiches and put
in a smelly half-eaten fish
from his pocket!
"If that doesn't make her cry at
school today, I don't know what
will!" he smirked, and dived back
down the plughole.

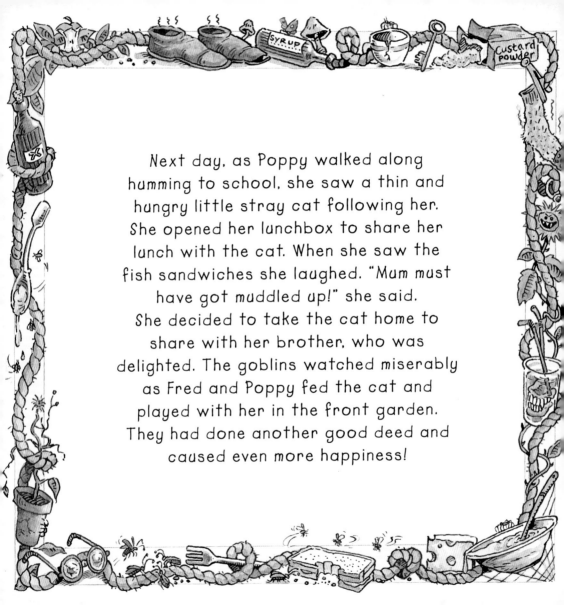

Next day, as Poppy walked along humming to school, she saw a thin and hungry little stray cat following her. She opened her lunchbox to share her lunch with the cat. When she saw the fish sandwiches she laughed. "Mum must have got muddled up!" she said.

She decided to take the cat home to share with her brother, who was delighted. The goblins watched miserably as Fred and Poppy fed the cat and played with her in the front garden. They had done another good deed and caused even more happiness!

That night, the goblins held
a special committee meeting.
They argued and shouted
and jumped up and down.
They boxed each others
ears. Finally they came to
a decision.
In the morning, Poppy
kissed her new cat goodbye.
She skipped along the
pavement, past the dark,
silent drain.

The goblins had gone.

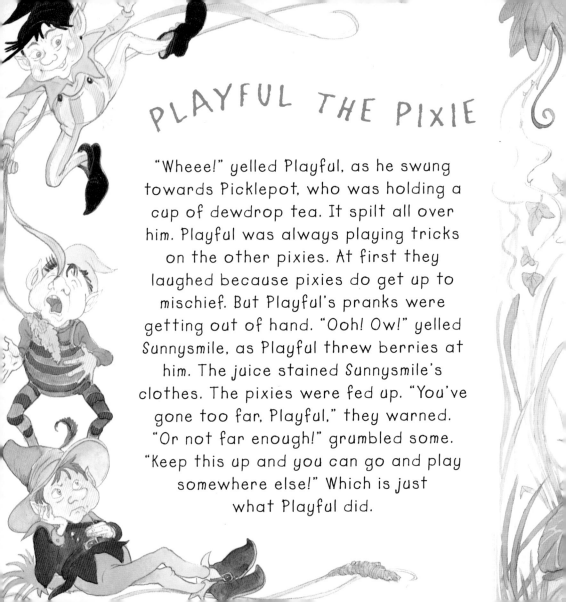

PLAYFUL THE PIXIE

"Wheee!" yelled Playful, as he swung towards Picklepot, who was holding a cup of dewdrop tea. It spilt all over him. Playful was always playing tricks on the other pixies. At first they laughed because pixies do get up to mischief. But Playful's pranks were getting out of hand. "Ooh! Ow!" yelled Sunnysmile, as Playful threw berries at him. The juice stained Sunnysmile's clothes. The pixies were fed up. "You've gone too far, Playful," they warned. "Or not far enough!" grumbled some. "Keep this up and you can go and play somewhere else!" Which is just what Playful did.

One morning, he set off early to a part
of the wood where a band of elves lived.
And what naughty tricks he played on
them! He hid and puffed pollen on the
elves to make them sneeze. While they
slept, he swapped their boots around
so they didn't fit! "This is more fun
than before," giggled Playful. "Now no
one knows it's me!"

That was until the elves caught him!
They knew someone was playing tricks,
so they laid a trap. The next time
he crept up on them a bag of
honey dropped on his hat and
burst open. "Caught you!"
they cried. "We're taking
you back where you
came from."

When Playful arrived home, the pixies were cross to hear about the trouble he'd caused. "The least we can do is invite you to a Pixie Party," Picklepot told the elves. "There'll be music and dancing!" And more of Playful's pranks. He put mud on the seats to make folk sit down with a squelch! Then he mixed up all the food and put mustard in the jam sandwiches and tomato ketchup in the sponge cake. Things had gone beyond a joke! So the elves and pixies made a secret plan...

Next morning, when Playful woke he had
a terrible shock. He was all alone in a
part of the wood he had never seen
before. As he sat up his blanket flew off
as if by magic. "What's happening?"
gasped Playful, reaching for his tunic.
But he couldn't put it on. It was much
too tiny! "That's not mine!"
he cried, crossly.
Then Playful spotted a piece of paper
with his name on it. As he went to pick it
up, a net hidden under some leaves
sprang up and closed around him, and
Playful found himself dangling in mid-air.
"Caught you!" cried a voice.
"Let me down! Please stop playing tricks
on me!" he called, feeling frightened.

"Only if you stop playing them on us!" said Picklepot, who stepped out from behind a tree with the other pixies and elves. "Yes! I promise!" said Playful. They lowered the net and helped him out. "It is not nice to be tricked, is it?" asked Sunnysmile sternly.

"No," agreed Playful, shaking his head. "From now on I won't play any more tricks. Except maybe just a small one, on Sundays." The elves and pixies chuckled.

From then on, Playful was the best-behaved pixie you could imagine. So if you ever meet a pixie, remember who it could be – but be careful never to ask him, "How's tricks?!" Especially on a Sunday!

A MONSTER HIT!

One day Kevin discovered a monster living in the television. He had just settled down to watch his favourite cartoon programme, 'The Adventures of Fancy Frog', with a huge glass of lemonade and a jumbo packet of crisps. Reggie the cat was sleeping on the rug, ears and whiskers twitching as he dreamed happily of chasing mice.

Kevin took a mouthful of crisps and a gulp of lemonade. Just then, a big hairy hand reached out of the back of the television and grabbed Kevin's crisps. The packet disappeared back into the television and Kevin couldn't hear what Fancy Frog was saying for the noise of crunching crisps!

Reggie opened one eye and his whiskers twitched. He had a feeling that there was another animal in the room. Kevin was cross about the crisps – and about missing his programme. It was just his luck to be the only boy in the street with a monster in his television.

Then just as he was about to drink his lemonade, the giant hairy hand shot out of the television and grabbed it! Glug, glug, glug went the television. Then it burped. "Mum!" shouted Kevin, feeling fed up. "Mum, there's a monster in the television and it's eaten my crisps and drunk my lemonade!" "Yes, dear," called Mum from the other room. "Your dad will fix it for you. "Kevin sighed. Dad had never been good at fixing things. He decided to call his friend Eric, who said he would come over and give him a hand.

When Kevin got back to the living room, Reggie was sitting on the top of the television with his head down and his nose pressed to the screen. Fancy Frog had disappeared and instead there was a huge, horrible, hairy monster face, grinning and poking its tongue out.

Reggie's fur was on end and he kept swiping at the face with his paw, but the monster was safely inside the screen. Then Grandma came in. She wanted to watch the weather, but the hairy monster was on every channel!

"Whatever is the world coming to?" she muttered.

The big hairy hand shot out of the television again and grabbed Reggie's tail. It swung him around then threw him on the sofa, where he landed in a heap. The face on the TV screen grinned. Reggie put his tail in the air and stalked out of the room. Just then, Eric arrived. They tried unplugging the TV, but the big hairy hand just shot out and plugged it in again. It was a real nuisance.

The word soon spread that there was a monster in the television at number 28. Before long there was a queue outside. Everyone wanted to have a look.

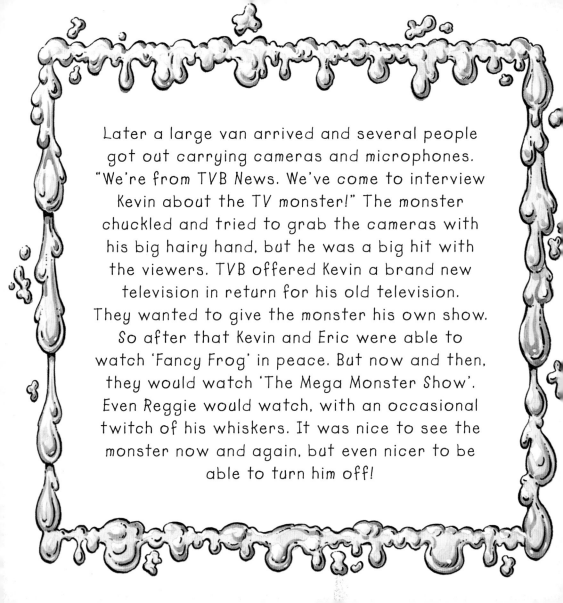

Later a large van arrived and several people got out carrying cameras and microphones. "We're from TVB News. We've come to interview Kevin about the TV monster!" The monster chuckled and tried to grab the cameras with his big hairy hand, but he was a big hit with the viewers. TVB offered Kevin a brand new television in return for his old television. They wanted to give the monster his own show. So after that Kevin and Eric were able to watch 'Fancy Frog' in peace. But now and then, they would watch 'The Mega Monster Show'. Even Reggie would watch, with an occasional twitch of his whiskers. It was nice to see the monster now and again, but even nicer to be able to turn him off!

The Mega Monster Show

Gnome Improvements

George the Gnome lived in a garden centre.
At night George and the rest of his gnome
friends played on the swings and slides
there and even swam in the pond. They had
lots of fun but were careful that nobody
saw them move, hurrying back to their
places before it got light. One day, George
overheard Sam, the owner, talking to
his assistant Sarah.
"The garden gnomes are not selling well,"
said Sam. "Let's put them on sale. Could you
paint a sign saying 'All gnomes half price'?"

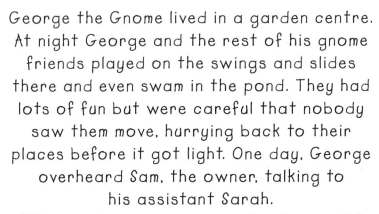

George was listening nearby. That night he called a meeting to tell the others what he had heard. "That's terrible," cried Grace. "If we all get sold to different people we'll never see each other again." "Don't worry," said George. "I've got an idea. Let's paint each other in lots of bright colours. We'll look so awful that nobody will want us!"

They all agreed it was a brilliant idea. George had seen where Sarah kept the paints and he went to fetch them. Throughout the night they had great fun painting each other in the brightest colours and most terrible patterns they could think of.

They just finished in time to get to their places before Sam and Sarah arrived. Sam took one look at the gnomes and let out a shriek.
"Aarghh, what's happened to the gnomes? We'll never sell them looking like that!" George winked at the others.
"Some kids must have got in last night and mucked about," said Sarah. All day long the customers remarked on how dreadful the gnomes looked. Then, just before closing time an old lady came through the gate.
"How wonderful," she cried when she saw the gnomes.
"I'll take one!"
Only one? The little gnomes panicked – who would she choose?

But the old lady couldn't choose. "I can't decide," she said, "So I'll take them all! I can't do much gardening any more, so I haven't got many flowers. These gnomes will add a splash of colour and make the garden look more cheerful." Sam could not believe his luck, and neither could the gnomes!

The old lady took the gnomes home, and soon
they were sitting in her lovely little garden.
She stood back to look at them.
"My you are colourful. You certainly brighten up
my garden. I hope you'll enjoy living here."

When the old lady went inside, the gnomes started to whisper in excitement.
"What a pretty garden," said Gilbert.
"There's a pond and a swing," said Gladys. "Probably for her grandchildren."
"Best of all, we're all together. I think we're going to be very happy here," said George, smiling.
When the old lady's friends saw the gnomes they wanted some too, so Sarah started to paint the new gnomes at the garden centre. They sold so quickly she could not paint them fast enough.
Sam was pleased as business had never been so good, and it was all because of the friendly gnomes who wanted to stay together.

THE GOOD GOBLIN

Deep in the heart of a great forest lived a gang of goblins. They were just like goblins everywhere – horrible. Small goblins went to school to learn how to be nasty. If a goblin passed all his exams he got a 'Certificate in Nastiness' and became a fully qualified goblin. But there was one goblin called Pookie who didn't quite fit in. He didn't like lying, stealing and playing naughty tricks, so he never passed a single exam. Pookie's problem was that he was just too nice! This week he had washed all the goblins' nasty, grimy clothes! He was impossible!

The others tried taking Pookie
to the goblin doctor.
"Can you give Pookie some medicine
to make him nastier?" they asked.
But although Pookie took his medicine
every day, it didn't make any difference.
"Come with us and pinch odd socks from
washing lines," said some
of the goblins.
"It's great fun!"
"No thanks," said
Pookie. "I'm helping
Mrs Squirrel move her
store of nuts."
"Come and rip holes
in shopping bags so
the food falls out!"
some others invited.

"Not today," said Pookie,
"I'm helping a blackbird build her
nest." And away he went, whistling.
Nothing seemed to work. There
was only one thing for it.
"We'll go and ask the wizard
to sort him out!" they cried.
"He's the only one who can
make Pookie nasty!"

Woozle the wizard lived in a cave near the forest. The goblins had often seen him mixing strange potions. They saw him turn a snail into a teapot and a rabbit into a toothbrush. Changing a nice goblin into a nasty goblin should be simple. They didn't know that Woozle wasn't very good at spells and was always getting mixed up! Luckily for the goblins the wizard had just turned his budgie into a chocolate chip cookie, so he was in a good mood. When they explained their problem, the wizard told them, "I'll be there tomorrow. Leave it to me!"

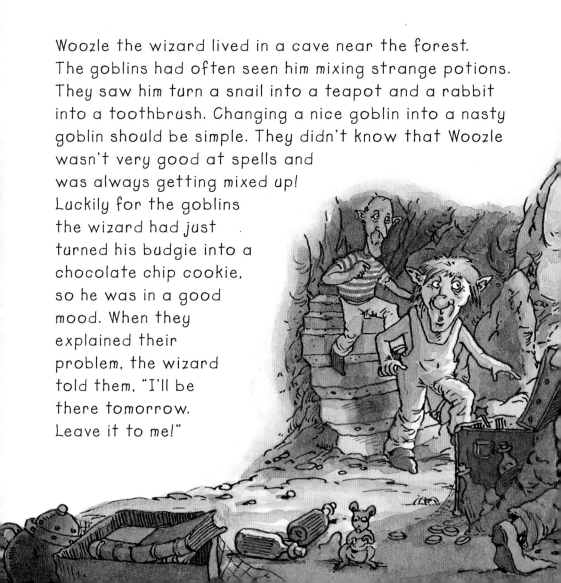

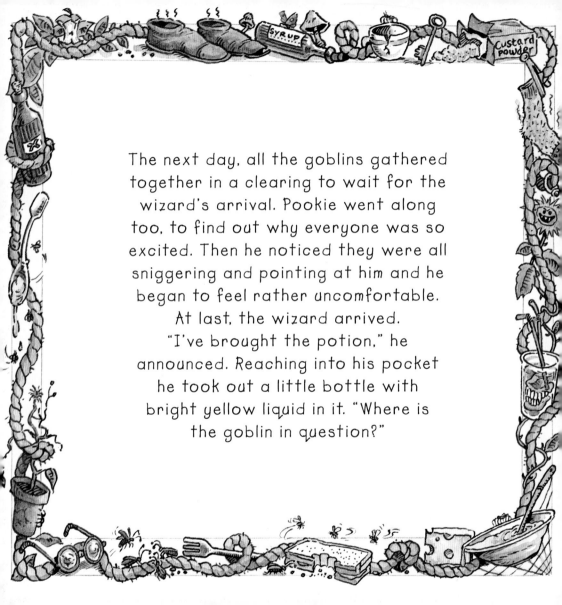

The next day, all the goblins gathered together in a clearing to wait for the wizard's arrival. Pookie went along too, to find out why everyone was so excited. Then he noticed they were all sniggering and pointing at him and he began to feel rather uncomfortable.

At last, the wizard arrived.

"I've brought the potion," he announced. Reaching into his pocket he took out a little bottle with bright yellow liquid in it. "Where is the goblin in question?"

Pookie was pushed forward. The wizard asked the other goblins to stand around him and hold hands. Then he sprinkled the yellow mixture around Pookie, and peered at a tattered piece of paper covered in scribbles.

"Here is nice where should be nasty, change this situation fasty!"

The wizard coughed nervously and looked at Pookie hopefully for signs of a sneer. But Pookie was looking at all the other goblins. They were dancing towards the wizard, hand-in-hand.

"Thanks so much for coming!" said one. "Please excuse us," said another. "We're just going to help some old ladies cross the road!" The goblins skipped away, stopping to pick daisies and wave at the butterflies. Pookie and the wizard stared at each other in amazement.

"That was a very good spell, Mr Wizard," said Pookie. "You must be the cleverest wizard in the whole world." Woozle thought it was a good spell to finish his wizard career. It was time to take up gardening.

TRADING PLACES

Katina hated being a pixie.
It was her job to look after the
woodland where she lived, but
Katina thought that was boring.
She wanted to be a Tooth Fairy.
Then she could dress in beautiful
fairy clothes and carry a wand,
some fairy dust, and a special
Tooth Fairy bag. Instead she had to
wipe the dew off the grass, polish
the leaves and paint the flowers.
She was so fed up and grumpy, that
no-one wanted to be her friend.
So she was lonely too.

One day, Katina was busy painting a
flower a nasty purple colour, when she
heard the sound of crying.
It was coming from a clump of
bluebells. Well, they would have been
blue if Katina hadn't painted them a
nasty green yellow.
Katina peeped behind them and
there was ... a Tooth Fairy!
"Gosh," said Katina. "A Tooth Fairy!
Why are you crying?"
"I've sprained my wing and I can't fly,"
said the fairy. "I was hurrying to visit
a little girl before she wakes up. She'll
be so disappointed if her tooth is still
there and there's no coin." The fairy
started crying again.

"I've got an idea," said Katina, as she helped the fairy out of the greeny-yellow bells. "I can fly, so I could take the coin to the little girl for you and bring you back her tooth!"

"All right," said the fairy. "There isn't much time though, and you must do exactly as I say."

She gave Katina careful instructions, handed her the special Tooth Fairy bag and sent her on her way.

Katina flew through the woodland bursting with joy. If she did this well, perhaps she would be allowed to become a Tooth Fairy one day.

The Tooth Fairy sat and waited, feeling worried, until Katina flew back panting, dirty and smelly! "I made it," she gasped, holding out the tooth bag.

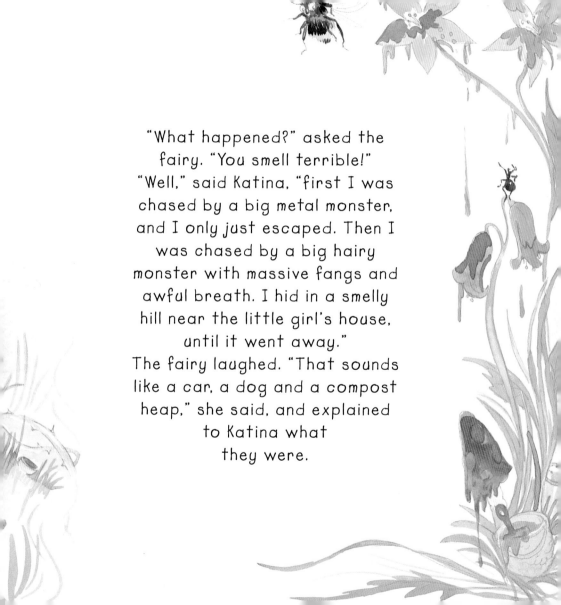

"What happened?" asked the fairy. "You smell terrible!"
"Well," said Katina, "first I was chased by a big metal monster, and I only just escaped. Then I was chased by a big hairy monster with massive fangs and awful breath. I hid in a smelly hill near the little girl's house, until it went away."
The fairy laughed. "That sounds like a car, a dog and a compost heap," she said, and explained to Katina what they were.

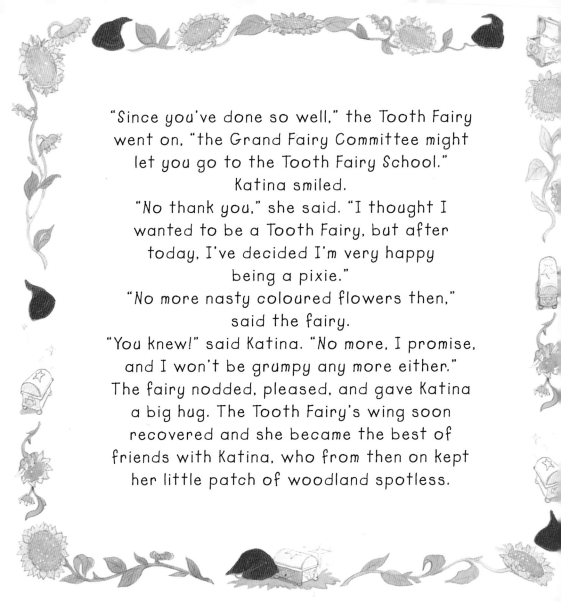

"Since you've done so well," the Tooth Fairy
went on, "the Grand Fairy Committee might
let you go to the Tooth Fairy School."
Katina smiled.
"No thank you," she said. "I thought I
wanted to be a Tooth Fairy, but after
today, I've decided I'm very happy
being a pixie."
"No more nasty coloured flowers then,"
said the fairy.
"You knew!" said Katina. "No more, I promise,
and I won't be grumpy any more either."
The fairy nodded, pleased, and gave Katina
a big hug. The Tooth Fairy's wing soon
recovered and she became the best of
friends with Katina, who from then on kept
her little patch of woodland spotless.

MONGO THE MONSTER

Katie was pulling monster faces in the mirror as she got ready for bed. She loved monsters. She had monster books, toys and a huge monster poster on her wall. While Dad read her favourite monster story, 'Mongo the Monster', she lay looking at her poster, wishing it was real and she could join the fun. She began to feel sleepy. She closed her eyes, and suddenly, she was standing behind one of the trees in the poster and could hear the monsters talking.

Katie peeked out at the monsters. They were very noisy, stomping about and making the funniest sounds. "Welcome to our Monster Competition," said Mongo to the others. "First of all it's the Monster Muscle Game." He explained they had to see who could throw a big rock the furthest.

The first monster lifted the huge rock high above its head and threw it into the air.

It landed by the tree, just missing Katie's foot. "Help!" she cried.

"What was that? Who's there?" asked Mongo.
"It's me," replied Katie creeping out from where she was hiding, and introducing herself. All of the monsters laughed because they thought she was a very funny looking creature.
"Pleased to meet you," said Mongo. "Why don't you join in our games?"
Katie was delighted.
One by one, the monsters threw the rock as hard as they could. Katie had a much smaller rock to throw.
The monsters cheered and said, "Well done. You're a great monster. You'll love the next game."

All the monsters, including Katie, had to stand in
the stickiest mud, and make a set of footprints.
Then they each had to guess which set belonged
to which monster. It was great fun, but they
all got in a terrible mess! Next came the
roaring game, each monster roaring
as loud as it could.
"Yaargh!" yelled Katie, and
everyone clapped.

Last was the funny face competition. Each monster took turns to pull silly faces. The monsters laughed till they cried when it was Katie's turn – imagine only having two eyes, one nose and one mouth! She won first prize and Mongo pinned a gold star onto her pyjamas. Then suddenly, there was a loud noise and Katie woke to find herself back in bed, her alarm clock ringing. But as she jumped out of bed she pricked her finger on something sharp. She looked down and saw the small gold star. She looked at her poster. All the monsters were there as before, as well as a small girl behind a tree.
"What have you been doing?" asked Mum, as she came in and saw Katie's muddy feet.
"Just dreaming," replied Katie, as she winked at Mongo.

Wonderwhiskers

Wonderwhiskers was a little gnome with
a very large beard. It was the thickest,
strongest and longest beard you could
imagine. He had tried cutting it, but by the
next day, it had always grown longer than
before. So Wonderwhiskers rolled it up under
his chin, and decided he'd just have to live
with it. Besides, he was proud of his beard.
It had made him famous!..

Once Wonderwhiskers had just been an
ordinary gnome called Norman. But then one
day Norman's beard had begun to grow and
grow. Every night he brushed his beard, and
measured it to see how much it had grown.
Such a big, bushy beard made him feel special.

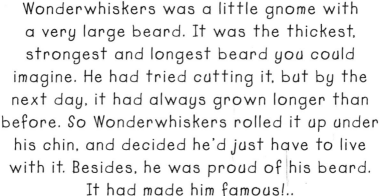

Soon word spread of his amazing beard, and visitors came from far and wide to see it. When Norman heard that King Cracklecorn was coming to visit he was very excited. "The king is coming to see my wonderful beard!" he boasted. But he was wrong. "Don't flatter yourself," said Tiggletum. "He's coming because *I* have something to show him!" Tiggletum had written to tell the king that he thought he had found the place where the rainbow ends. He had seen a beautiful rainbow, with one end disappearing deep in the forest. Soon the king arrived to join the search for the pot of gold at the rainbow's end.

By the time they had searched through half the
forest and walked in circles for a few hours,
everyone was feeling grumpy, especially the king.
To make things worse, it began to rain hard.
Then, as they hurried home beside the river, the king
had an accident! He slipped on the wet grass, fell in
and was nearly washed away. "Someone fetch
a rope!" yelled Tiggletum, as King
Cracklecorn clung to a rock.
"We don't have a rope!
We don't have anything that can
save him!" cried Bizzybonce.

"Oh, yes we have!" replied Norman. He unrolled his beard and threw the end to the king who managed to grab it. "Hold on, your Majesty!" called Norman. Turning to the others, he said, "Hurry! Help me pull him towards us!"

Inch by inch, through the swirling water, the King of the Gnomes was pulled closer.

Norman closed his eyes, bit his lip and never made a sound, although it must have been very painful. After all, imagine how hard his beard was being tugged!

Ouch!

But, at last, the little gnomes lifted the weary king out and he sat puffing on the riverbank. Soaked but safe, he turned to Norman.

"I hereby name you Wonderwhiskers," he said, "and grant you the title of S.M.I.G!"

"Second Most Important Gnome!" whispered Tiggletum to the others. "That means only the king is more important than Norman, I mean Wonderwhiskers, now!" All the gnomes thought he had been very brave and clever. And from that day on, he spent his time enjoying one visit after another, to tell his famous story and show off his amazing beard.

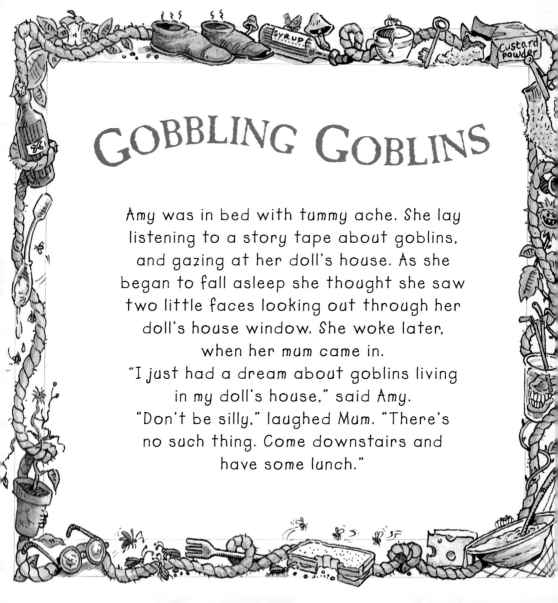

GOBBLING GOBLINS

Amy was in bed with tummy ache. She lay
listening to a story tape about goblins,
and gazing at her doll's house. As she
began to fall asleep she thought she saw
two little faces looking out through her
doll's house window. She woke later,
when her mum came in.
"I just had a dream about goblins living
in my doll's house," said Amy.
"Don't be silly," laughed Mum. "There's
no such thing. Come downstairs and
have some lunch."

"Eat up," said Mum, putting an egg and bread soldiers in front of Amy. "But I don't feel hungry," whined Amy. Just then the phone rang and her mum went to answer it. Amy blinked in surprise as two goblins ran out from behind the pepper pot. "We'll eat it!" they said, and in no time at all they had eaten Amy's lunch all up! They ran back to their hiding place, giggling. "Well done!" said Mum, coming back and seeing Amy's empty plate. "I didn't eat it. It was the goblins hiding behind the pepper pot," said Amy. "Very funny," said Mum. "You'll feel better now you've eaten."

Amy lay watching television, but after a while she felt hungry, and asked her mum for something to eat.
"You just had lunch!" said Mum.
Amy tried hard to explain that the goblins really had eaten her lunch, but her mum wouldn't believe her.
In the end her mum got cross and sent her up to her room for telling fibs.
Amy lay down on her bed and started to cry. She was amazed when Munch and Crunch, the goblins, crept out from the doll's house.
"You do live there, after all!" she said.
The goblins felt very bad for getting her into trouble, and promised to make it up to her.
"Wait there," said Munch.

Munch and Crunch went and fetched trays of plastic food from the doll's house kitchen. "I can't eat that," laughed Amy, "it's not real." But Munch and Crunch held hands and muttered a magic spell. With a flash, a real feast appeared. Amy happily tucked into sandwiches, cakes, crisps, sausage rolls, biscuits and ice cream.

"I hope you enjoyed our lunch," said Crunch.
"Oh, I did. It was much nicer than a boiled egg," said Amy and they all laughed. They said goodbye and the goblins disappeared back into the doll's house.

Amy was just licking the last bit of ice-cream from her lips when Mum came in with a tray of food.

"I thought that you might want some tea and biscuits," said Mum.

"Yes, please," said Amy. Just then the phone rang and Mum went to answer it. When she came back all the biscuits had gone.

"Who ate all those?" asked Mum.

"I did," replied Amy. "The goblins have gone home."

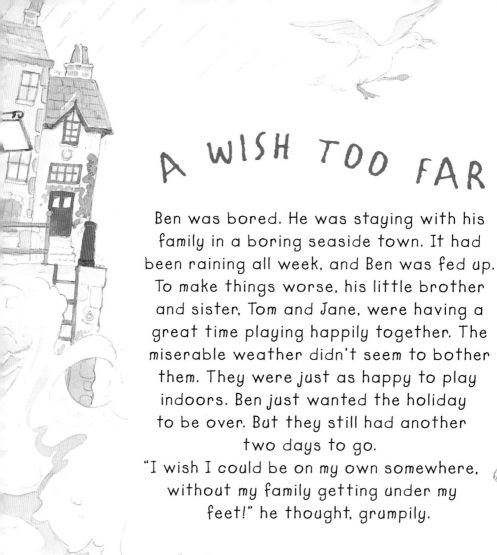

A WISH TOO FAR

Ben was bored. He was staying with his family in a boring seaside town. It had been raining all week, and Ben was fed up. To make things worse, his little brother and sister, Tom and Jane, were having a great time playing happily together. The miserable weather didn't seem to bother them. They were just as happy to play indoors. Ben just wanted the holiday to be over. But they still had another two days to go.

"I wish I could be on my own somewhere, without my family getting under my feet!" he thought, grumpily.

He put his coat on and went out into the garden. But Jane and Tom were following him.

"Why don't you leave me alone?" he snapped.

"We want to see what you're doing!" Tom replied.

"I'm not doing..." Ben began, but was cut off as he disappeared from sight. He had fallen down a big hole. He climbed back out holding a small, shiny box.

"Look what I found down there!" said Ben. Just then, the box slipped from his hand and landed on the wet grass. The lid flipped open and a tiny man appeared. He hung in the air before landing on a nearby flower. "Ohhhh..." he groaned. "My aching back! I've been in that box for years!"

"Who are you?" asked Ben.
"I'm Eric the Elf!" he said, proudly.
"You have freed me from a trap set a long time ago by a very grumpy wizard! In return I will grant you three wishes!"
Without thinking, Ben said, "I wish my family would disappear!"
In a flash, Jane, Tom and their parents vanished.
"I'm a busy elf!" said Eric.
"What's your second wish?"
"I wish I was somewhere nice and hot, all by myself!" Ben answered.
And suddenly, he was alone on a beautiful beach. "Wow!" Ben said.
"This is brilliant, eh, Eric? Eric?" but there was no answer.

Ben ran around for what seemed
like ages, but the empty beach
appeared to have no end, and
the forest behind the beach
looked a bit dark and scary.
Finally, hot, tired and worried, he
sat down on the sand and
began to cry. If only he
could be back with his
family in that wet
seaside town!

"Is that your third wish?" asked
a little voice, making him jump.
It was Eric.
"You said you wanted to be
alone, so I gave you a
little time to yourself!"
"Well, I wish I was
back with *my*
family!" Ben said.
"I'll see what
I can do,"
said Eric.

Jane tugged at his arm and Ben felt the rain on his face. "Come on!" she said, as she and Tom peered down at him. Ben climbed out of the hole and looked around, feeling very glad to be back. He could see his mum and dad inside. "Your brother and sister won't remember me!" Eric said, appearing in front of him. "But I think you will, and you'll remember what you learnt today!"

"I will!" Ben said. "I'll never take my family for granted again!"

And as Eric twinkled from sight, Ben looked up at the grey sky, took his sister's hand, and ran inside laughing to join his family!